A Christmas Guest

A Christmas Guest

by **David LaRochelle**
illustrations by **Martin Skoro**

Carolrhoda Books, Inc./Minneapolis

This book is available in two editions:
Library binding by Carolrhoda Books, Inc.
Soft cover by First Avenue Editions
241 First Avenue North
Minneapolis, Minnesota 55401

Library of Congress Cataloging-in-Publication Data

LaRochelle, David.
  A Christmas guest.

  Summary: A young child and his mother help an old woman seeking a bit of warmth on Christmas Eve, only to find out later that she was a very special guest.
  [1. Christmas – Fiction. 2. Stories in rhyme]
I. Skoro, Martin, ill. II. Title.
PZ8.3.L327Ch   1988   [E]   88-18927
ISBN 0-87614-325-7 (lib. bdg.)
ISBN 0-87614-506-3 (pbk.)

Manufactured in the United States of America
    4 5 6 7 8 9 10 98 97 96 95 94 93 92

To Kathy Haubrich

One cold and blowy Christmas Eve when I was not so old,
when the wind was full of frostbite, and the sky was thick with snow,
I snuggled warm beneath my quilt with dreams of Christmas day,
until a knock at our front door swept all those thoughts away.

I heard Mom on the stairway, and hurried to her side.
The cold floor sent me hopping as my bare feet tried to hide.
Mom yawned and opened up the door; we looked outside with care.
Just take a guess at what you think it was I saw out there...

I heard the wind, I felt the cold, I *saw* a tiny lady.
Her face was drawn with wrinkles; she looked seventy – or eighty.
Her legs were bare as icicles, her hair was crowned with frost.
Her coat was thin and raggedy. I guess her gloves were lost.

"May I come in?" she asked my mom, "and warm my hands and toes?"
She winked at me and shyly said, "I think I froze my nose!"
Mom was sleepy; I could tell she wished she were in bed.
This lady should have knocked upon our neighbor's door instead.
At last Mom smiled and said, "Come in," and drew her in with haste,
then went to light a crackly fire in our fireplace.

The lady huddled near the fire, reaching toward the heat.
The flames began to thaw her hands and warm her frozen feet.
"That's better now," she said to me; her face looked warm and pink.
"But the blizzard's still inside me. Have you something hot to drink?"

There was a box of cocoa that I'd hidden on a shelf,
a box of thick hot chocolate I'd been saving for myself.
I thought a bit, then finally said, "I'll have to check and see."
I got the box and came back in, with mugs for her and me.

At last the lady took my hand and gently squeezed it tight.
"You're very kind," she told me. "Now it's time I said good-night."
She wrapped her coat around her and turned slowly toward the door.
I caught her arm and whispered, "Could you stay a minute more?"

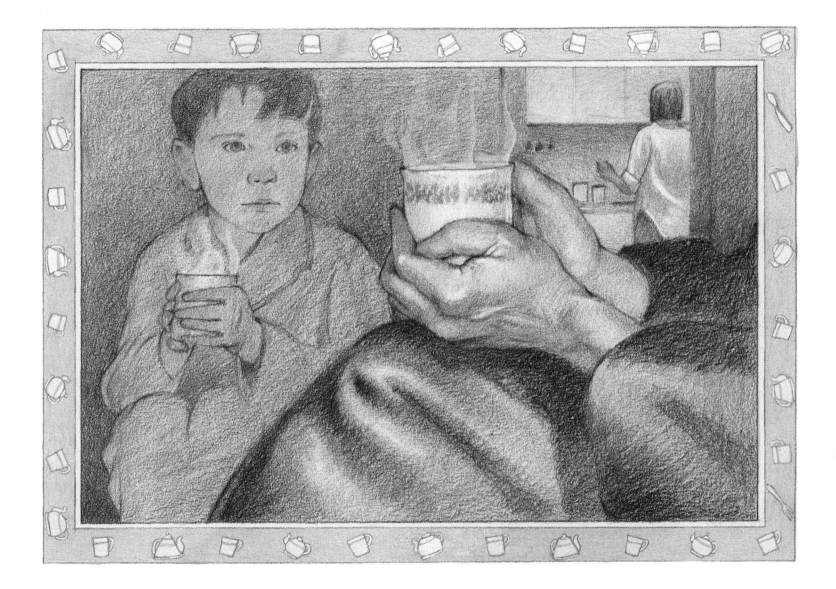

I opened our front closet door and climbed up on a chair
and searched until I found my scarf, my favorite thing to wear.
I gave it to the lady. "This is soft," I said, "and warm.
The cold will not come near you when you go out in the storm.
"Merry Christmas," I wished her. She smiled at me once more.
"Merry Christmas," she said warmly, as she stepped beyond the door.

The house was quiet. So was I. But then my mother said,
"Your bedtime, dear, is long since past. You'd best get back to bed."
With thoughts of our strange visitor, I headed up the stairs,
and when I stopped to look outside, I saw a wonder there!

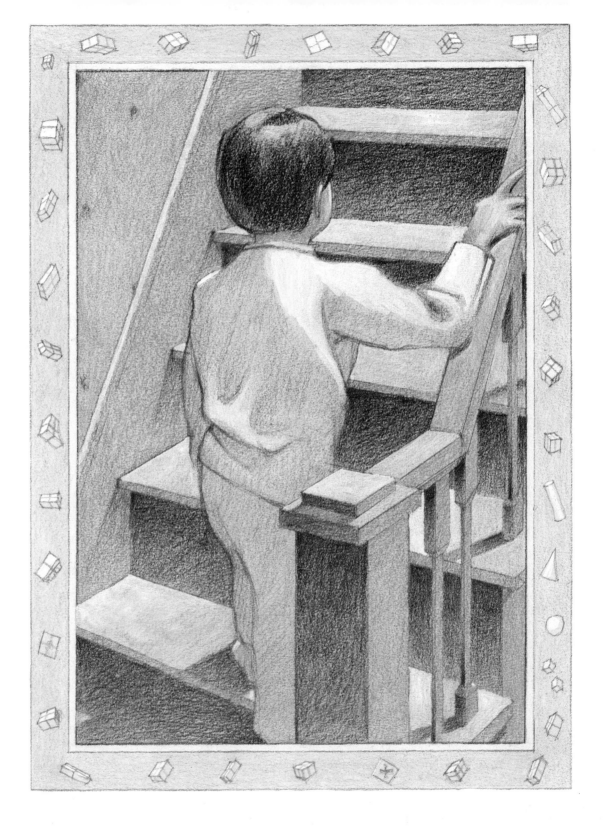

Amid the whirling snowstorm, in the nighttime, in the cold,
I saw an angel like a star, all dressed in light and gold.
Her sudden brilliance lit the dark, her presence filled the night,
and there, around the angel's neck, my scarf danced wild and bright.

In seconds she had vanished. I wondered what to do.
I'd never had an angel visit me before – have you?
I pressed against the window; at last I shook my head
and decided that it might be best to go on up to bed.

But when I reached my room I was amazed at what I found:
there on my bed a wooden box, with ribbons wrapped around.
I slowly lifted up its lid, and then my eyes grew wide;
a tiny angel made of gold lay glittering inside!

Now every year at Christmastime, when winter winds blow cold,
I place high on my Christmas tree that angel made of gold.
I sip a mug of cocoa as I gaze up at the tree,
and think about the angel who spent Christmas Eve with me.